THE UGLY DUCKLING

Adapted by Katharine Ross

Illustrated by Bernhard Oberdieck

A Random House PICTUREBACK® READER

Random House 🏠 New York

Text copyright © 1991 by Random House, Inc. Illustrations copyright © 1991 by Bernhard Oberdieck. All rights reserved under International and Pan-American Copyright Conventions. Published in the United States by Random House, Inc., New York, and simultaneously in Canada by Random House of Canada Limited, Toronto. Library of Congress Catalog Card Number: 90-61004   ISBN: 0-679-81039-0

Manufactured in the United States of America   2 3 4 5 6 7 8 9 10

Once upon a time,
some ducklings hatched.

"You are not
like the others,"
said the mama.

Honk!

Peep! Peep! Peep!

"You are an ugly one,"
said the mama.
"Ugly duckling! Ugly duckling!"
said the others.

The ugly duckling
ran away.

"Why am I so ugly?"
the ugly duckling asked the lake.
"Who knows?" said the lake.

"Why am I so ugly?"
the ugly duckling
asked the wild ducks.
"Who knows?"
said the wild ducks.

"Why am I so ugly?"
the ugly duckling
asked the dog.
The dog ran away!

"Why can't I be beautiful
like the swans?"
"Who knows?"
said the wild, wild wind.

"Who knows why
you are so ugly?"
said the man.
"But my children
like ducklings."

"Ugly duckling! Ugly duckling!"
said the children.
The ugly duckling ran away.

The ugly duckling grew...

and grew...

and grew!

"Why can't I be beautiful like you?"
said the ugly duckling.
"But you <u>are</u> beautiful,"
said the swans.

"Am I beautiful?"
asked the ugly duckling.

"Yes," said the lake.

"Yes," said the dog.

"Yes," said the children.

"Yes, yes, yes!"
said the wild, wild wind.
"You are a beautiful swan."

Why did a swan
hatch with some ducklings?
Who knows!

Turn the page for mini learning cards. Instructions on the inside of the back cover of this book will tell you how to use them with a child.

MINI LEARNING CARDS

See the Note to Parents on the inside back cover for ways to use the cards with your child.

a	dog	man	the
am	duckling	my	time
an	ducklings	not	ugly
and	ducks	once	upon
are	grew	one	who
asked	hatch	others	why
away	hatched	peep	wild
be	honk	ran	wind
beautiful	I	said	with
but	knows	so	yes
can't	lake	some	you
children	like	swan	
did	mama	swans	